The **Little** Green **Island**
With a **Little** Red **House**

May you always love the little things!

A **Book** of **Colors** *and* **Critters**

by Sharon Lovejoy

Sharon Lovejoy

Down East Books

Camden, M___

Published by Down East Books
A wholly owned subsidiary of The Rowman & Littlefield Publishing Group, Inc.
4501 Forbes Boulevard, Suite 200, Lanham, Maryland 20706
www.rowman.com

Unit A, Whitacre Mews, 26-34 Stannary Street, London SE11 4AB

Distributed by NATIONAL BOOK NETWORK

Library of Congress Control Number: 2014944933

ISBN 978-1-60893-464-5 (cloth : alk. paper) —ISBN 978-1-60893-465-2 (electronic)

∞ ™ The paper used in this publication meets the minimum requirements of
American National Standard for Information Sciences—Permanence of
Paper fo   inted Library Materials, ANSI/NISO Z39.48-1992.

      r Darul Ehsan Malaysia – November 2014

For my favorite
little nature lovers...
Sara May, Moses, and Luke Arnold,
Ilyahna and Asher Prostovich,
Logan Burgess,
Evan and Tessa Borchardt,
Sydney and Dylan Watt,
Sammy Rae and Justine Means,
and Noah Gelinas.

, Maine

On a little green

island

stands a little red

house

with a little orange

cat

a little gray

mouse

a little rose

moth

a little beige

bat

who sleeps
upside-down
on a little

hat rack

And beneath the shaggy
edge of a little purple

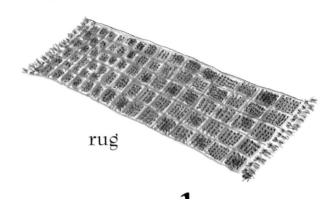

rug

it has a roly-poly
polka-dotty

little copper

bug

The little green

island

has a little chartreuse

frog

who searches for his
supper on a little mossy

log

It has a leafy little peach

tree

a little mocha

mole

a little ochre

cricket

who peeks out

from a h●le

It has a little patch
of violets

in a shady little glen

and a little
russet

fox

with three

kits

inside her den

The little green

island

has a little lilac

shell

and a little cobalt

bird

with a voice
just like a

bell

It has a

little olive

snail

with a

little slimy

tail

who s l i t h e r s
through the

forest

on a
slippery, shiny trail

The little green

island

has a little khaki

toad

a little yellow-sided

snake

who basks along
the road

It has a little azure

butterfly

and a little
white-striped

skunk

who spends
all her days
in a little plum

tree's

trunk

The little green

island

has a little scarlet

newt

who lives all alone
in a little rubber

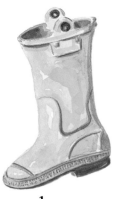

boot

It has a little chestnut

chipmunk

and a little

saffron

spider

who bundles
up her little

eggs

and keeps them
close beside her

The little green

island

has a little black-rumped

bee

a little pink-tongued

porcupine

who hangs
out in a

tree

And in a little silver

tide pool

by the sparkling
sapphire

sea

the little green

island

has a someone
just like me!

Faretheewell

Dear Reader,
And now it's
time to stop &
Look — for
Colors found
outside your
book!
Sharon Lovejoy